Two and Two
Are Four

Two and Two Are Four

Carolyn Haywood

Illustrated by the author

AN ODYSSEY/HARCOURT YOUNG CLASSIC

HARCOURT, INC.

Orlando   Austin   New York   San Diego   Toronto   London

Requests for permission to make copies of any part of the work
should be mailed to the following address: Permissions Department,
Harcourt, Inc., 6277 Sea Harbor Drive, Orlando, Florida 32887-6777.

www.HarcourtBooks.com

First Odyssey/Harcourt Young Classics edition 2005
First published 1940

Library of Congress Cataloging-in-Publication Data
Haywood, Carolyn, 1898–1990.
Two and two are four/Carolyn Haywood; illustrated by the author.
"An Odyssey/Harcourt Young Classic."
p.   cm.
Summary: When Teddy and Babs move from a city apartment
to a home in the country, they share an exciting summer with
two children who are visiting at a neighboring farm.
[1. Country life—Fiction.]   I. Title.
PZ7.H31496Tw   2005
[Fic]—dc22   2004060557
ISBN 0-15-205230-5   ISBN 0-15-205231-3 (pb)

Text set in Bodoni Classico
Designed by Kaelin Chappell

Printed in the United States of America

A C E G H F D B
A C E G H F D B (pb)

To
Jessie Wilcox Smith
Violet Oakley
and
Elizabeth Shippen Green Elliott

CONTENTS

Two and Two Are Four

1

Floppy Ears and Whiskers

Timothy Edward was six years old. He was named Timothy after his great-grandfather Baker and Edward after his great-grandfather Robinson. Great-grandfather Baker always called him Timothy and great-grandfather Robinson always called him Edward, but everybody else called him Teddy.

Teddy had a little sister who was four years

old. Her name was Sarah Elizabeth. She was named Sarah after her great-grandmother Baker and Elizabeth after her great-grandmother Robinson, but everybody called her Babs because she was the baby.

Teddy and Babs lived in a big city that was full of high buildings very close together. They lived with their daddy and mother in a big building that, Teddy said, wasn't so very high. Babs said, "No, but it isn't so very low." It was called an apartment house.

Teddy and Babs didn't live in the whole house but in a little part of it behind a door that had "11 A" painted on the outside. "11" meant that it was on the eleventh floor and "A" meant that the Robinsons lived there and not in "11 B" where Mr. and Mrs. Jenkins lived and not in "11 C" where Miss Horner lived.

When Teddy and Babs wanted to go out to play they had to push a button in the wall between two doors in the hall. Then they would wait and watch the hand on the clock over the door. It moved slowly; "1, 2, 3, 4, 5, 6, 7, 8, 9, 10, 11," they would say. Then the door would open and there was the elevator to carry them down to the ground. Sometimes it was James who ran the elevator and sometimes it was Bill.

Teddy and Babs would say, "Hello, James," or "Hello, Bill," and the elevator boys would say, "Hello, Teddy and Babs." The boys were always glad to see Teddy and Babs, but they were never glad to see what Teddy and Babs had with them, for they always had their tricycles or their scooters or their skates. Sometimes Teddy had his express wagon and Babs had her doll coach and all of these things took up a great deal of room in the elevator. Teddy and Babs thought it was a nuisance too, and they wished that they could leave all of their playthings downstairs right by the front door. Daddy said, "That wouldn't do at all," and Mother said that was the trouble with living in an apartment house.

Teddy and Babs didn't have any yard to play in, but they played in a big square that was across the street from the apartment house. All of the children who lived in the apartment houses around the square played there. It was a pretty square with cement walks and trees and grass and flower beds and a fountain with a pool where they could float little boats.

There was a statue of a billy goat in the square, too. He was made of bronze. Every day Teddy and Babs climbed upon his back and

took a make-believe ride. The billy goat's horns and the top of his head shone like a bright new penny because all of the children who played in the square stroked him and patted him, and this made him very shiny in the patted places.

Teddy and Babs rode their tricycles on the cement walks, but they couldn't run on the grass or climb the trees or pick the flowers or go wading in the pool, and these were the things Teddy and Babs wanted very much to do. They wanted to almost as much as they wanted a puppy dog to play with, but Daddy said you couldn't have a dog in an apartment. It was bad enough having tricycles and scooters and express wagons and doll coaches. So Teddy and Babs patted the billy goat and wished for a puppy dog.

One day Teddy had a new boat. It was a sailboat. It was bright green on the outside and bright yellow on the inside, and it had a mast with two little white sails. There was a tiny red flag flying from the top of the mast. Teddy thought it was the most beautiful boat he had ever seen. He sat on the side of the pool and floated the boat, but there wasn't any breeze to move it across the pool. Teddy leaned over and blew the little boat. Away she went! When the boat stopped, he leaned over farther and blew her again. She sailed farther away. All the children stopped to look at Teddy's boat. This made Teddy feel very proud. He wanted his boat to go faster so he leaned way over the side of the pool and blew as hard as he could. He blew so hard that he lost his balance and *Ker-Flop!* went Teddy over the side of the pool right into the water.

"Oh! Oh!" shouted all of the children.

"Oh! Oh!" cried Babs, jumping up and down. "Teddy fell in! Teddy fell in!"

A little red-and-white spaniel and a little brindle Scottie dog began to bark very loud. They ran up and down and barked and barked.

Michael, the policeman, came running from the other side of the square. When he saw Teddy sitting in the pool and looking very scared, he cried, "Now, now, I'll get you out. You're not hurt a bit, but you sure do look wet. Haven't I told you to be careful when you float those boats?"

Michael lifted Teddy out of the pool and squeezed some of the water out of his little trousers and sweater. "Sure, if it hadn't been for the little dog calling me," said Michael, "you would have drowned for certain." All the children came running to the pool. They watched Michael take off his big coat and wrap it around Teddy. Then the policeman picked him up and carried him across the street into the apartment house. Babs ran after him carrying the little sailboat. When they stepped into the elevator, Bill said, "What happened, Teddy?"

Michael said, "Man overboard, that's all."

"Teddy blew too hard," said Babs.

Teddy was still so scared he didn't say anything.

When Michael handed him over to his mother,

Mrs. Robinson thanked the policeman again and again. Michael said he was glad he happened to be nearby and he didn't care if his coat was a little damp.

Teddy's mother took off Teddy's wet clothes and gave him a hot bath. Then she tucked him in his bed where it was nice and warm. Soon he was sound asleep.

That night at dinner Daddy heard all about how Teddy fell into the pool.

"It was that little spaniel with the floppy ears that saved my life," said Teddy. "He barked so loud Michael heard him."

"No, no, Teddy, it was the Scottie dog. He barked much louder," said Babs.

"No, it wasn't," said Teddy. "It was the little spaniel."

"I ought to know," said Babs. "I was on the outside. You were in the water and you couldn't hear."

"Yes, I could," replied Teddy. "We'll have a little dog someday, won't we, Daddy?"

"Someday," said Daddy, "when we live on a farm."

"It will be a spaniel with floppy ears, won't it, Daddy?" said Teddy.

"Ah, no, Daddy," said Babs. "I want a little Scottie dog. Scottie dogs have such nice whiskers."

"We'll see," said Daddy. "We'll see when we live on a farm."

"What is a farm?" asked Teddy.

"A farm," replied Daddy, "is a great big piece of ground with a lot of grass and trees and flowers, where you grow corn and wheat and hay and all kinds of vegetables, where there are cows and chickens and pigs and horses and a house without an elevator where you can leave the toys by the front door."

"Can you run on the grass?" asked Babs.

"Can you climb the trees?" asked Teddy.

"Can you pick the flowers?" asked Babs.

"Yes," replied Daddy, "you can do all those things."

"Oh, Daddy!" cried the children. "Let's live on a farm."

"Yes," said Mother, "let's."

One day Daddy came home from the office early. His face was all shiny with a surprise. "Pack up your overalls!" he shouted. "We are moving to a farm."

"Where there is grass and trees to climb?" cried Teddy.

"And flowers to pick and chickens and little pigs?" asked Babs.

"And a house with a front door to leave the toys beside?" asked Mother.

"Yes, yes," cried Daddy, "and a farmer who lives in the house across the road to do the farming."

"What will you do, Daddy?" asked Teddy.

"Oh, I'll catch trains to the city," replied Daddy, "and work in the office and think of you and Babs and Mother feeding the chickens and milking the cows, and then I'll catch another train home in the evening just in time to tuck the chickens and the cows into bed."

"Will there be a Scottie dog?" asked Babs.

"No, there will be a spaniel with floppy ears, won't there, Daddy?" said Teddy.

"Now that is one thing I forgot to find out," answered Daddy.

At last the day came when Teddy and Babs and their mother and daddy rode down in the elevator for the last time. They were off to the farm. They drove in Daddy's car miles and miles out into the country. Every time they passed a farm, Teddy and Babs would call out, "Is this it, Daddy?" and Daddy would say, "No, it's nicer than that."

Finally they reached the farm. The house stood on the side of a hill with the grass rolling down to a meadow. The grass was green and velvety smooth. The children ran on it shouting with glee. "Can we roll on the grass, Mother?" cried Teddy.

"Yes, indeed," said Mother, "roll."

Teddy and Babs lay down on the grass and rolled over and over all the way down to the meadow. Then they sat up and looked up into the branches of a big apple tree. "It's fun to live on a farm, isn't it?" said Babs.

"I'm going to climb that apple tree this afternoon," said Teddy.

"Urf, urf!" came a sharp bark from the house and down the hill to the children scampered a red-and-white spaniel puppy.

"Oh!" cried Teddy, as he took the puppy in his arms, "I told you it would be a spaniel. Look at his floppy ears."

Babs looked at the puppy. He was sweet and soft and silky and his big brown eyes were sad. But she did so want a Scottie. Babs' eyes were as sad as the puppy's and two big tears began to roll down her cheeks.

"Yip, yip!" came another sharp bark and down the hill rushed a little brindle Scottie. Babs jumped up and caught the puppy. She held him close to her cheek. She loved his rough coat. "My Scottie dog!" she said. "My Scottie dog with whiskers!"

2

It's Fun to Slide on the Banister

Teddy and Babs loved the farm. There was the stone house to live in and there was a big barn and a stable. The house seemed very big to Teddy and Babs after living in the apartment, and it had a great many doors and windows. The driveway led up to a white door with a shiny brass knocker, but there were stepping-stones that led around to the other side of the house and there was a porch and another white door. This door had a bell that you pulled.

Teddy and Babs couldn't agree about the front door. Teddy said that the door with the knocker was the front door, and Babs said that the door with the bell was the front door. When they asked Daddy about it, he said, "Let's have two front doors. After all, anybody can have one front door, but it is very special to have two front doors." So they called them "the knocker front door" and "the bell front door." There was a side door, too, and a back door, and pretty soon there were toys beside every door. Finally Daddy fell over them once too often and then he built a closet under the stairs. It was called "the toy stable" and Teddy and Babs had to put their toys in the stable when they were through playing with them.

Teddy and Babs thought the stairs were the nicest part of the house, for they had never had stairs before. The stairs were long because the ceilings were very high and it took a great many steps to reach from the first floor to the second floor. Of course with so many steps there was a long banister rail and Teddy and Babs thought this was the most fun of all. They sat on the banister at the top and slid down to the bottom over and over again. Sometimes they slid down separately and sometimes they slid down together. Sometimes they came down backwards and sometimes frontwards and every once in a while they discovered a new way to slide down the banister. Sometimes Daddy or Mother would say, "No, no! Not that way," and Teddy and Babs would have to give up their brand-new discovery.

Teddy and Babs spent hours playing on the stairs. There were so many games to play. Sometimes they were animals in the zoo and they looked out between the bars and roared terrible roars. Sometimes they made believe that the staircase was a hill and they tobogganed down to the bottom. Sometimes it was a train with dolls and stuffed animals traveling to the city, but Teddy and Babs agreed that the most fun was to slide down the banister.

One day the painter came to paint the woodwork in the hall. He painted all of the posts white, and the banister he painted a beautiful dark brown. When the painter went home at the end of the day, it looked so beautiful and clean that Mother was delighted. "Now remember,"

she said to Teddy and Babs, "you must be very careful not to touch the wet paint. It takes two days for the paint to dry."

Teddy and Babs said that they would remember and trotted off to bed.

The next morning when they came downstairs, Babs said, "Don't touch the paint, Teddy. It's wet."

"I know it's wet," said Teddy. "You don't have to tell me."

After breakfast, Mother said, "Who wants to go to the village with me to get the mail at the post office?"

"I do! I do!" cried Babs.

"Are you coming, too, Teddy?" asked Mother.

"No," replied Teddy, "I'm very busy. I'm building an airport for my airplanes."

Mother and Babs drove off and left Teddy alone. After a while he went upstairs to get a piece of string that was in his little desk drawer. He stuck the string in his pocket and trotted off. "This is a wonderful airport that I am building," thought Teddy. "Mother and Babs will be surprised when they come home and see what I have made. And I'll keep it to show to Daddy, too."

When he reached the head of the stairs, Teddy threw his little leg over the banister and *Zoop!* down he went to the bottom. There he stopped. Instead of getting off as he always did, he sat very still. Something was the matter and the matter was that Teddy was stuck. He was stuck to the banister. He looked at his hands. His palms were covered with brown paint. He looked at the banister. All the way down the banister there was a light streak where Teddy had wiped off the paint. Very carefully he pulled himself loose. There was a sticky noise as though the banister didn't want to let Teddy go. His blue linen trousers felt very wet and sticky, for all the paint that had been on the banister was now on the seat of his little trousers.

Teddy went upstairs to the bathroom. He washed his hands with soap. He rubbed them very hard, but they stayed dark brown. Then he took off his trousers. Out of his bureau drawer he took another pair of blue linen trousers just like the ones he had spoiled. He put them on and buttoned them to his white shirt. Then he picked up the painty trousers and hid them on the floor of the closet, way back in the corner where it was very dark.

As he went down the stairs he looked at the banister. "It doesn't show very much," thought Teddy. "Maybe Mother won't see it."

Somehow, he didn't want to go on building his airport. Something made him want to get out-of-doors and away from the house. So, without telling Mary, the cook, where he was going, he ran down the hill and across the meadow to the brook. There he floated leaves and sticks and made believe they were boats racing.

After a while, Mother and Babs came home. Mother went upstairs to take off her things. She looked at the banister and she saw the streak running from the top to the bottom and she saw the finger marks but she didn't say anything.

It was almost lunchtime when Teddy came back to the house. "Hello, Teddy," said Mother, "did you have a nice morning?"

"Uh-huh," murmured Teddy.

"Did you finish your airport?" asked Babs.

"No, I didn't," replied Teddy.

When lunch was ready, Mother said, "Teddy, are your hands clean? Let me look at them."

Teddy turned his palms upward. They were still very brown.

"My goodness!" said Mother. "What dirty hands!"

"They get awful dirty playing around," said Teddy.

"They certainly do," replied Mother. "Go and wash them."

Teddy washed his hands. Again he rubbed them very, very hard and he used a great deal of soap, but it was no use. They were still brown.

He slid into his place at the table and kept his fists clenched all through lunch.

"Why didn't you finish your airport?" asked Mother.

"Oh, I just didn't want to," replied Teddy.

As soon as lunch was over, he ran back to the brook. He spent the afternoon building a dam out of stones.

Babs played with her dolls on the living-room floor. Once she said, "Mother, I wonder where Teddy is."

"I wonder!" replied Mother.

Late in the afternoon the painter returned. He painted the banister all over again with dark-brown paint. Then he put a big sign at the top of the stairs and a big sign at the bottom of the stairs. The signs said WET PAINT.

Teddy came back just before dinner. He was very quiet.

That night when Mother gave him his bath, Teddy wondered why Mother scrubbed the place where the seat of his trousers went so very hard. She had never scrubbed him so hard there before, and she used a great deal of soap. After he was all dry, he put on his pajamas. Mother heard him say his prayers. He jumped into bed and Mother tucked the covers all

around him. Then she sat down on the edge of his bed.

"Teddy," she said, "isn't there something that you would like to tell Mother?"

Teddy was very quiet. He was quiet a long time. Mother sat waiting. She hummed a little tune.

At last Teddy said, "I didn't do it on purpose, Mother. I just forgot about the paint and when I remembered, I was down at the bottom."

"I see," said Mother. "Is there anything else?"

"Yes," said Teddy, "my trousers are on the closet floor, way back in the corner."

"I'll get them," said Mother. "I'm glad you told me, Teddy." And she kissed her little boy good night.

3

Buried Treasure

Mr. Perkins was the farmer who did the farming for Teddy and Babs's daddy. He lived with Mrs. Perkins in the house across the road. Teddy and Babs loved Mr. and Mrs. Perkins. Mr. Perkins gave them each a small piece of ground for a garden, and he showed them how to dig it and turn the ground over with their little spades. Then be showed them how to break up the ground and make it all crumbly and soft. Teddy and Babs each had a little rake and a little hoe just like Mr. Perkins' big rake and hoe. When the ground was ready, he gave them each some seeds to plant. There were carrots and beets and radishes and, because Babs wanted some flowers in her garden, they planted some zinnia seeds and some nasturtiums. Mr. Perkins said, "The twins always have a garden. The twins will be here soon for their vacation. You'll like the twins."

Mrs. Perkins let Teddy and Babs come into her big kitchen when she baked cakes and pies. She would give Babs a little piece of dough and a tiny pie plate. Babs would roll the dough very thin and put it in the pie plate. Then Mrs. Perkins would fill it up with apples or berries or custard and bake it in the oven beside her big pie. The children would sit in the kitchen waiting for the little pie to bake. When it came out of the oven, they could hardly wait for it to cool off, so that they could have a tea party.

When Mrs. Perkins made a cake, she let Teddy and Babs lick the batter that stuck to the sides of the bowl. Mrs. Perkins said, "The twins always like to lick the bowl, too. It won't be long now before the twins come."

One day Babs said to Teddy, "Teddy, what's twins?"

"I don't know," replied Teddy.

"Well, twins are coming to the Perkins'," said Babs.

"I know," said Teddy, "but I don't know what they are."

That very afternoon when Teddy and Babs went over to see Mrs. Perkins, they found a little girl and a little boy in Mrs. Perkins's kitchen. Mrs. Perkins was making a cherry pie. The little girl was rolling out a piece of piecrust just the way Babs had done before. When Mrs. Perkins saw Teddy and Babs, she said, "Oh! here are Teddy and Babs. These are the twins," she added, pointing to the little boy and girl. "They are our grandchildren. Their names are Peter and Jane."

Peter and Jane said, "Hello," and Babs and Teddy said, "Hello."

"Here, Babs," said Mrs. Perkins, "here is a piece of piecrust for you to roll. There is only one little pie plate so you and Jane will have to make cherry dumplings and bake them in the same pan." So Babs and Jane took turns rolling their piecrust. Mrs. Perkins gave them some cherries and they each made two little dumplings so that they could each have one.

"Do you want to see my knife, Teddy?" asked Peter.

"Yes," said Teddy.

Peter took a brand-new knife out of his pocket. It was made of horn and it had two blades. "You can hold it," said Peter. Teddy held it and thought it was a wonderful knife.

"Do you know how to whittle?" asked Peter.

Teddy shook his head.

"Well, some day I'll teach you how," said Peter.

Teddy thought Peter was nice to show him his knife and to offer to show him how to whittle.

When the cherry dumplings were baked a golden brown, Babs said, "Let's go out under the pear tree and have a party."

"It has begun to rain," said Mrs. Perkins. "You will have to stay indoors."

"Oh, Granny!" cried Jane. "Can we go up in the attic and have our party?"

"Yes," said Mrs. Perkins, "run along."

The children scampered up the stairs to the very top of the house. Teddy and Babs had never been in the attic before. They thought it

was a wonderful place. It was a big room and the roof went up into a peak in the center and sloped right down to the floor on the two sides. At each end there was a window shaped like a half moon. The patter of the rain on the roof was very loud and they could hear the water rushing along the gutters of the roof. The attic was filled with a great many things. There were some old tables and a big bedstead all in pieces. There were trunks and boxes and barrels. There was an old spinning wheel and some stuffed birds in a glass case.

Peter and Jane pulled a little table into the center of the room. Then they found a stool and a tiny chair. These they gave to Babs and Teddy because they were guests. Peter sat on an old chest and Jane sat on a pile of magazines. Then they ate their cherry dumplings.

"What is in all those trunks?" asked Teddy.

"Oh, quilts and clothes and things," answered Jane.

"Do you ever open them?" asked Teddy.

"Sometimes," replied Peter. "Sometimes we get dressed up."

"Let's get dressed up now," said Jane. "Get

up, Peter, you're sitting on the chest that has our dress-up clothes in it."

Peter got up and the children knelt down beside the chest. Jane lifted the lid. A faint musty odor came from the inside of the chest. Teddy's and Babs's eyes were big and round as they watched Jane lift a faded blue silk dress out of the chest. "You can put this on, Babs," said Jane.

Then she pulled out a pair of blue trousers and a coat with brass buttons. It was a soldier suit.

"I want to wear the soldier suit," cried Peter.

Teddy felt a little sorry because he would have

liked to wear the soldier suit, but he didn't say anything.

"I'll wear this green silk with the black lace on it," said Jane, as she laid the dress on the floor.

"Oh, look, Teddy! Here's a little boy's suit. I'll bet it will just fit you."

Teddy didn't think it was much fun to wear a little boy's suit when there was a soldier suit to wear, but he put it on. First he put on the little white shirt. It had a collar of embroidery. Then he put on the tan wool trousers. They were very full like balloons and fastened tightly around his ankles. There was a short purple velvet jacket, just the color of ripe plums.

"I feel funny in these clothes," said Teddy. "You couldn't climb trees in these trousers." He sat down on a trunk and watched Peter put on the soldier suit. It was a man's suit. When Peter put it on, the coat came down to the floor, so he didn't bother to put on the trousers. Jane and Babs trailed up and down the room in their long ladies' skirts and made curtsies to each other. Teddy put his hands in the pockets of the tan trousers. He pushed them down as far as they would go. They were very deep pockets. Way down in the bottom of one of the pockets

he felt a piece of paper. He pulled it out. It was yellow from age and very soiled. "Look what I found," said Teddy.

"What is it?" said Jane.

"It's a piece of paper," said Teddy.

The children crowded around Teddy as he unfolded the paper.

"Oh, look!" said Peter. "There is a drawing on the paper and some writing. Let's show it to Grandaddy."

Teddy led the way down the attic stairs. The other three trailed their clothes behind them.

Grandaddy was in the kitchen. When he saw the children, he said, "Here comes the big parade."

"Look, Grandaddy, look at what Teddy found in the pocket of those trousers," cried Jane.

"It's a paper with writing on it," said Babs.

"I'll bet it's important," said Peter.

Grandaddy took the paper. He put on his spectacles and looked at it very hard. "Well, well!" he said. "This says that this is a map showing the place where there is buried treasure."

"Oh, Grandaddy, where is it?" cried Jane.

"I told you it was important; I'll bet it belonged to Captain Kidd," said Peter.

Mr. Perkins began to read. "Go to the cherry tree beside the barn," he read aloud. "Face the pump and take five steps forward. Under your feet you will find buried treasure."

The children's eyes were nearly popping out of their heads. "Let's go find it," they shouted.

"You will have to wait until it stops raining," said Grandaddy. "You can't go out in this weather."

It rained all day and all night. The children talked of nothing but the buried treasure.

The next morning the sun was shining. Before breakfast Teddy and Babs were over at Mr. Perkins's house with their spades. The four children trotted off to the barn. When they got there, they couldn't find the cherry tree.

"That's funny," said Peter, "there isn't any cherry tree here."

Just then Mr. Perkins appeared. "Grandaddy," cried Jane, "there isn't any cherry tree."

Mr. Perkins pointed to a tree stump. "I guess that is it," he said. "That cherry tree was cut down years ago."

"That's it, then," said Teddy and everybody felt more cheerful. The children faced the pump. Then they took five steps, and all began to dig. They had not been digging very long when Teddy's spade struck something hard. "I've found it," he cried, "I've found the treasure!" But when he lifted his spade it was just a stone. The children went on digging. At last Jane's spade struck something hard. She knelt down on the ground and felt in the hole with her hands. "Here's something," she cried. All the children fell to their knees beside her. Jane pushed some more earth aside. Sure enough, there was the top of a little iron chest. It was covered with rust. Peter lifted it out of the hole. It was no bigger than a doll's trunk.

"Open it! Open it!" cried Teddy.

Peter tried to open it but the lock was too rusted to move.

The children ran to Mr. Perkins with their treasure. "Here it is, Grandaddy," they shouted.

Mr. Perkins took the chest and with a hammer finally loosened the lock. Peter lifted the lid. "Ah!" sighed the children as they gazed upon the treasure. There was a very old penknife, a string of blue china beads, a doll's cream pitcher and sugar bowl, and an envelope containing two copper coins. On one side of the envelope there was a name and address. The ink was brown and faded. In the corner there was a stamp.

"Oh, boy!" cried Peter. "Look at that stamp. It's a real old one. I'll put that in my stamp book."

On the other side of the envelope, in big round letters, were the words, "This treasure was buried by Captain Kidd Perkins, September 12th, 1853."

"Why, this chest must have been buried by

my father when he was a little boy," said Mr. Perkins. "He must have been playing 'Pirates.'"

"Is it all ours?" asked Jane.

"Yes, you found it," said Mr. Perkins, "but Teddy found the map, so he should have first choice of the treasure."

Teddy immediately chose the knife, and Peter took the stamp and the copper coins. Jane wanted the blue beads and Babs wanted the doll's cream pitcher and sugar bowl. So everyone was happy.

"I'm glad I wore that little boy's suit," said Teddy. "Now I can whittle."

4

A Fourth of July Picnic

Not far from the Robinsons' farm was a wide river. Running along beside the river there was a narrow stream. It was separated from the river by a strip of land covered with beautiful trees. As Teddy looked at the river and the stream, he thought they looked just like a big mother river with a little baby river, but Daddy said that the little river was not a river at all. It was a canal.

"Why is it a canal?" asked Teddy.

"A canal is built," replied Daddy, "while a river is made by many little streams flowing together."

"What do they use the canal for?" asked Babs.

"They send things from one place to another up and down the canal," answered Daddy. "The boats are called barges. Perhaps if we wait a little while, we'll see a canal barge."

They walked down to a small wooden bridge that crossed the canal. The children leaned over the side of the bridge and looked at their reflections in the still water. Once Teddy dropped a pebble into the water. It made rippling circles.

The children laughed when they saw their faces all full of ripples.

Just then they heard the tinkle of a bell. It didn't bongle like a cowbell and it didn't jingle like a sleigh bell. This was a tinkling bell.

"What is that bell, Daddy?" asked Teddy.

"A barge is coming now," said Daddy. "That is the bell on the mules that you hear."

"The mules!" exclaimed Babs. "I didn't know mules pulled boats. I thought they only pulled wagons."

The children peered ahead. They couldn't see anything, but the sound of the bell was growing louder.

"Oh, Daddy!" said Teddy. "Do the mules swim in the water?"

"No," laughed Daddy, "they walk along that path beside the canal." Daddy pointed to the narrow path that ran close beside the water. "That is called the towpath," he said.

Soon the barge appeared. The children could see it, piled high with sand. Now they could see the mules plodding along the path. They pulled the barge very slowly by a long rope. A young boy stood on the barge. As it passed under the bridge, Teddy and Babs waved their hands. The boy waved and called, "Hello."

"Oh, Daddy!" cried Teddy. "I wish I could ride on a canal barge. It goes so smooth and silky."

"Yes," said Babs, "it would be nice to ride on one."

"I'll tell you what we'll do," said Daddy. "I'll hire a canal barge on the Fourth of July and we'll go on a picnic."

"With Mother, too?" asked Babs.

"And the twins?" said Teddy.

"Yes," answered Daddy, "we'll take Mother and the twins, and perhaps Mr. and Mrs. Perkins will come, too."

"That will be fun!" cried Babs.

"Maybe I can ride on one of the mules," said Teddy.

"We'll see," said Daddy.

The children could hardly wait for the Fourth of July to come. Every evening Teddy stood on a chair in the kitchen and put a big black cross through the date on the calendar. Then he would say, "Only eight more days until the Fourth of July." The next day he would say, "Only seven more days until the Fourth of July." At last the

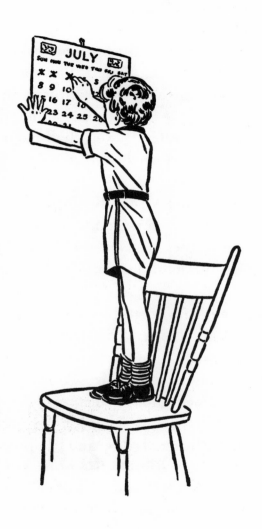

evening came when he said, "Only one more day until the Fourth of July."

All that day Teddy and Babs and the twins were busy getting ready for the picnic. Mrs. Perkins baked cookies, and Babs and Jane helped her to cut the thin dough with little tin molds. There were hearts and diamonds and circles and rings. There were half-moons and clovers. They were sprinkled all over the top with chopped nuts.

Peter and Teddy drove into town with Mr. Perkins in the station wagon to get all the good things that Mother had ordered for the picnic supper. Teddy's mouth watered as he saw them all.

"We mustn't forget to buy some apples, Mr. Perkins," said Teddy. "We have to have an apple for each of the mules that pull the barge."

"Sure enough!" said Mr. Perkins. "Some apples and some lumps of sugar for their picnic supper."

That night, after Teddy and Babs were in bed, Babs called to Teddy from her bed in the next room. "Teddy," she said, "do you know what I am going to take on the picnic?"

"What?" asked Teddy.

"Some saltwater taffy," she replied.

"Where did you get it?" said Teddy.

"I saved it out of the box that Aunt Ethel sent us from the seashore."

"How many pieces have you?" Teddy asked.

"Four," replied Babs. "They're chocolate."

"Can I have one?" asked Teddy.

"Yes," said Babs. "I'll give one to Peter and one to Jane, too. Aren't you glad they are chocolate?"

"Uh-huh," murmured Teddy in a very sleepy voice.

The next morning the children were up bright and early. They ran over to see if the twins were ready, long before Mother and Daddy were down to breakfast. All morning the children kept saying, "Aren't we going soon, Daddy?" "Is it almost time to go, Mother?"

At last it was time to go. "Where is the lunch basket?" asked Teddy.

"Mr. and Mrs. Perkins are bringing it in the station wagon. Mr. Perkins can't leave the farm so early," said Mother. "We will ride on the barge to the covered bridge. Mr. and Mrs. Perkins will meet us there and ride with us to the end of the canal. Then we will eat our supper and come back in the moonlight."

The four children trotted off with Mr. and Mrs. Robinson. They walked to the canal. There was the barge tied up to the landing. The mules were nibbling the grass by the side of the towpath. The boy who had waved to Teddy and Babs the first time they had ever seen a canal barge was waiting for them. His name was James.

"How would you like to ride one of the mules a little way?" he asked Teddy.

"I'd like that," replied Teddy.

The boy lifted Teddy up on the mule's back while the others settled themselves on the barge. Soon they were off, gliding slowly up the canal. They passed little houses whose gardens came right down to the edge of the water. They could almost pick the flowers. The trees arching overhead made it cool and green. The sun shone through the leaves and made bright speckles on the water. Birds sang in the trees. *Tinkle, tinkle, tinkle,* went the bell. *Clop, clop, clop,* went the mules' feet.

After a while Teddy came on the barge and Peter rode on the mule. Then Babs and Jane each had a ride.

At last they reached the covered bridge. The

children strained their eyes to be the first to catch a glimpse of Mr. and Mrs. Perkins.

"I don't see them, Mother," said Teddy.

"Well, they must be here somewhere," replied Mother. "There is a car coming down the road to the bridge now." But the car went over the bridge.

"That is strange," said Daddy, "they should have been here by this time."

"Perhaps this is the car," said Jane. Another car came down and passed by. Another and another came. They all passed on. The barge waited a long time.

At last James said to Mr. Robinson, "I'm sorry, sir, but we'll have to go on without them. We are due at the end of the canal now and I have to bring another party back."

"All right," said Mr. Robinson, "we'll go on."

"Without our supper!" cried the children. "What will we do without our supper? We can't have a picnic without our supper!"

"Don't worry," said Daddy. "Mr. and Mrs. Perkins will probably find us."

"Giddyup!" said James. The mules started again. The barge glided away from the covered bridge. After what seemed a long time to the children, they reached the end of the canal.

They were beginning to feel very hungry as they stepped off the barge.

Another picnic group scrambled on the barge. Soon Teddy and Babs and the twins and Mr. and Mrs. Robinson were alone, sitting on the bank of the canal. The children looked longingly after the barge. The people on the barge had such a big picnic basket and they had none. Perhaps Mr. and Mrs. Perkins wouldn't find them, they thought. Then they would have nothing to eat. Babs thought of her chocolate saltwater taffies. She hoped nothing would happen to them.

Daddy walked up to the road to see if he

could see anything of Mr. and Mrs. Perkins. He watched for them a long time. At last he said, "I guess we will have to find a hot-dog stand."

"Oh, dear!" sighed Babs. "Our lovely supper with cookies and everything!"

"Never mind!" said Mother. "We can have a good time eating hot dogs. It can't spoil our fun."

The little group started to walk up to the road. The children's faces didn't look very happy.

Suddenly, Peter cried, "Oh, look! Here come Grandmother and Grandaddy now!"

"Oh, Grandaddy!" cried Jane. "We thought you were lost!"

"Have you got the supper?" asked Babs.

"Course he's got it," said Teddy. "Can't you see the basket?"

"We had engine trouble," said Mr. Perkins. "Couldn't get the car started. We had to come in the bus."

"We thought we would find you before it got dark," said Mrs. Perkins.

Babs and Jane helped to unpack the supper basket and everyone sat down on the grass.

How the children ate! Mrs. Perkins said that she thought the sandwiches would come right out of the children's eyes.

Just at dusk the barge returned to take them home. Teddy gave the mules each an apple and Peter gave them some sugar. The mules enjoyed their picnic supper, too. Then they all went on the barge. Mr. Perkins carried the empty picnic basket on board. The children were sleepy now. No one wanted to ride on the mules. They lay down on some blankets and looked up at the stars peeping through the leaves. The barge floated slowly through the darkness. Tiny lights shone fore and aft, like giant fireflies.

"It's like fairyland," whispered Jane.

Clop, clop, clop! Tinkle, tinkle, tinkle!

5

Cowboys Are Brave

Teddy and Peter were sitting on the back porch of the Perkins house. They had played hard all day. Now dinner was over and each little boy had his penknife and a piece of wood. Peter was trying to teach Teddy how to whittle. "You should see Grandaddy whittle," said Peter. "He can make the chips go anywhere he wants to. Grandaddy learned to whittle when he was a cowboy. He says all cowboys are good whittlers."

"Your grandaddy was a cowboy?" said Teddy.

"Sure he was a cowboy," replied Peter. "He lived on a big ranch."

"You mean he was a real cowboy," said Teddy, "with whiskers on the sides of his pants?"

"Yes, and spurs on his boots and a hat that would hold a gallon of water," said Peter.

"It did?" gasped Teddy, his eyes as big as saucers. "And did he have a long rope to catch the cows?"

"You bet," replied Peter, "and he caught other things beside cows."

"What other things?" asked Teddy.

Peter leaned over and looked right in Teddy's face. "Horse thieves!" he said. "Outlaws who used to come and steal the horses at night."

"Oh!" said Teddy. "They were bad men, weren't they?"

"Yes," said Peter, "and there were coyotes, too. They used to steal the sheep. Grandaddy says you could hear them howling at night."

"I'm going to be a cowboy when I grow up," said Teddy. "I wouldn't be afraid of the coyotes and I'd like to see any old thief steal my horses.

I'd lock him up in jail and I wouldn't let him have any dessert." Teddy thought it would be terrible never to have any pudding.

"Oh, you have to be awful tough and awful brave when you're a cowboy," said Peter, shaking his head.

"I tell you what," said Teddy, "let's play we are cowboys."

"All right," said Peter, "let's."

The next morning Teddy came down to breakfast with the fringe from an old automobile robe pinned to the sides of his overalls. Around his neck he wore one of the cook's brightly printed handkerchiefs.

"Look at Teddy," cried Babs, as Teddy came into the dining room.

"Howdy, pardner!" said Daddy. "How's the cowboy this morning?"

Teddy was pleased that Daddy knew that he was a cowboy without being told.

"Are you a cowboy?" asked Babs.

"Of course he is a cowboy," said Daddy. "You can tell by the spinach hanging on his trousers."

"I want to be a cowboy, too," said Babs.

"You can't be a cowboy," said Teddy. "Girls can't be cowboys."

"But I don't look like a girl in my overalls," pleaded Babs.

"Well, there isn't any more fringe and you can't be a cowboy without whiskers on your pants."

"I could make believe I had whiskers on my pants," said Babs.

"Well," replied Teddy, "I'll have to ask Peter when he comes."

It was time for Daddy to leave for the station. He kissed Mother and Babs good-bye. Then he shook hands with Teddy. "So long, pal," he said.

"So long," replied Teddy. Teddy was glad Daddy hadn't kissed him. He didn't think cow-boys should be kissed.

Just then Peter galloped up to the side door. He was wearing one of Grandaddy's old felt hats. "Whoa!" cried Peter and he climbed off a make-believe horse.

"Howdy, pardner!" said Teddy, as he came out to greet Peter. "Lose any horses last night?"

"See, Teddy!" cried Babs, "Peter hasn't any whiskers on his pants. Now can I be a cowboy?"

"Shall we let her be a cowboy, Peter?" asked Teddy.

"Can you catch horse thieves?" Peter asked, looking hard at Babs.

"Yes," answered Babs, nodding her head very hard.

"Are you afraid of coyotes?" he asked.

"No," she replied, shaking her tiny braids.

"All right," said Peter, "you can be a cowboy, but if you get scared you can't play."

Just then Jane dashed up. "What are you playing?" she cried.

"We're not playing," said Peter. "We're cowboys and we are after a horse thief. One of the best colts was stolen out of the corral last night."

"You mean one of Grandaddy's colts?" cried Jane.

"No," replied Peter, "we're just making believe."

"Oh," said Jane, "I'll bet it was that thief. The one with the evil eye."

"Sure it was!" cried Peter. "Come on, boys! To horse!"

The children mounted their make-believe horses and galloped down the road in a cloud of dust. They galloped hither and yon, all morning. There were sounds of *Bang! Bang! Bang!* and shouts of "To horse, boys!" "The dirty thief!"

The chase had to be interrupted for lunch and the cowboy with the whiskers on his pants ate three dishes of pudding. Then the children had their afternoon nap. By four o'clock the hunt was on again, but by dinnertime the thief had not been captured. Teddy was sure he had seen him riding over the top of a hill and Peter was certain that he had heard the report of the thief's gun.

After dinner Peter said, "Know what we ought to do tonight?"

"What?" chorused the others.

"We ought to sleep in the barn," he whispered. "Then if the horse thief came again, we could grab him."

"That's right," said Teddy.

"Well, let's sleep in the barn," said Jane.

"Babs," said Peter, "you can't sleep in the barn, because you are the baby and you would get scared."

"No, I wouldn't," said Babs.

"Yes, you would," said Teddy. "You would be scared of the coyotes. They howl in the middle of the night."

"I won't get scared," said Babs. "I want to sleep in the barn." She began to cry.

"Oh, all right," said Peter, "but remember, if you get scared, you can't be a cowboy."

The children asked if they could sleep in the barn. It was a clear, warm night and Mother and Daddy said they could. Off they dashed to make up their beds in the hay. Floppy and Whiskers, the two dogs, went with them. Soon they were all curled up for the night. At first there was a great deal of whispering, then one by one they dropped off to sleep.

"Hoo! Hoo! Hoo!" hooted an owl in a nearby tree.

Teddy woke up. *"Hoo! Hoo! Hoo!"* he heard. Teddy began to tremble. *"Hoo! Hoo! Hoo!"* *Perhaps it isn't an owl,* thought Teddy. *Perhaps it's a coyote.* He felt stiff and chilly. He wished that he was in his own little bed. *"Hoo! Hoo! Hoo!"* Teddy felt for his shoes. He picked them up and tiptoed out of the barn. Then he ran as fast as he could until he reached the side door. It was unlocked. He tiptoed up the stairs and crawled into his bed. He couldn't hear the coyote now. He felt much better. Soon Teddy was sound asleep.

After a while Jane woke up. The moon was gone now and it was pitch dark. She heard a noise in the loft overhead. She was sure it was a bat. Jane didn't like bats. She wished that she were home where there weren't any bats. She sat up. There was the noise again. Without thinking of her shoes she dashed out of the barn door, through the flower garden, across the road and upstairs to her own room. The bed felt nice and soft and smooth.

Soon it began to rain. The patter of the rain on the roof of the barn woke Peter. A door was banging in the wind. It was a scary sound. Peter wished that it would stop. *Bang! Bang! Bang!* went the door. It was pouring now. Peter wished that he were home. *Bang! Bang! Bang!* He forgot all about the horse thief. It was cold. He peered around in the darkness. He couldn't see the other children. He guessed they were all asleep. Tiptoeing to the door, he looked out at the pouring rain. Then he made a dash for home. When he reached his room, he pulled off his wet clothes and slid in between the nice dry sheets on the bed.

Toward morning a farmer's dog began to howl. He was locked out. *"Youl! Youl! Youl!"* he went. The sound was awful. Babs woke up, startled. *"Youl! Youl! Youl!"* she heard.

"Teddy," she whispered, "is that a coyote?" There was no answer.

"Teddy! Peter!" she called.

"Youl! Youl! Youl!" was all she heard.

Babs sat up. The dawn was just breaking. There was a faint light in the barn. She rubbed her eyes and looked around her. She saw that the others were gone. She was alone! Just as she was beginning to feel very frightened, she looked down. Pressed close beside her little legs were Floppy and Whiskers. She picked up the sleepy little dogs and tucked them up close to her body. She put her arm around them. They felt warm and soft. The howling had stopped now. In a few moments she was asleep again.

When she woke up, Mother was standing in the doorway with an umbrella. "Darling," she said, "were you frightened?"

"No, Mother," replied Babs. "I'm a cowboy. Cowboys are brave."

6

Shorty Goes to the Horse Show

One Saturday afternoon Teddy and Babs went into town with Daddy. When they arrived they found that there was a circus in town. It wasn't a big circus, like the one that came to the city once a year, but just a little circus. There was a merry-go-round and the music made a cheery sound. There was a peanut and lemonade stand and a man who sold balloons.

Bright-colored pennants fluttered from the sides of the tent. A man sat at the entrance to the tent selling tickets. A crowd of boys and girls swarmed around him.

Teddy and Babs rode on the merry-go-round and Daddy bought them each a balloon.

"Can we go inside the tent and see the circus?" they asked.

"Well," said Daddy, "I guess we may as well make a day of it."

The children were delighted as they skipped along toward the circus tent.

Inside of the tent there was a large space shaped like a ring. It was sprinkled with sawdust. Outside of the ring there were rows of seats. The seats were rapidly being filled with boys and girls. Some of the little children were with their mothers and fathers, others were with big brothers and sisters. The children were all very happy. They called to each other and waved their hands. They clapped for the circus to begin and stamped their feet. At last the performance began. First the clowns came out and chased each other around the ring. One of the clowns stood on his head and played an accordion. Then there was a juggler who kept ten balls in the air all at once and never dropped one. After the juggler, there were trained dogs. Then acrobats appeared in pink tights.

At the very end of the performance there were three trained ponies. Teddy and Babs had never seen such lovely ponies. They were not much bigger than large Saint Bernard dogs. They were black-and-white and their shaggy manes were

braided with red ribbons. The ponies jumped through hoops and over hurdles. They shook hands and counted by nodding their heads. When their names were called the ponies made deep bows. Their names were Shorty, Snorty, and Porty. Someone started to play an accordion and the little ponies began to dance. They danced all around the ring, lifting their tiny feet and keeping time to the music.

The children were delighted with the ponies and clapped very hard when they took their last bows.

"My, but I wish we could have a little pony, just like those little ponies!" said Teddy as he came out of the tent.

"I like the littlest one best," said Babs.

"His name is Shorty," said Teddy.

"Maybe someday we can have a little pony like Shorty," said Babs.

"Do you think we could, Daddy?" asked Teddy. "I would take good care of him, I would."

"Perhaps," answered Daddy. "Perhaps, someday, you can have a pony. But you must not expect him to do all of the things that the circus ponies do."

When the children reached home, they told Mother and Peter and Jane all about the circus. They talked a great deal about the ponies.

"Daddy says maybe he will buy us a pony," said Babs.

"And I'll bet I could teach him to do tricks," said Teddy.

One afternoon Teddy and Babs were playing a game of croquet with Daddy on the front lawn. Just as Teddy was about to knock Daddy's ball away from the last wicket, a big truck turned in at the drive.

"Oh, look!" cried Babs. "Look at the pony in that truck."

Teddy dropped his mallet and ran toward the truck. It had stopped now, right by the stable. The driver was climbing down.

"Oh, Daddy," cried Babs, "are they bringing the pony to us?"

"Looks that way, doesn't it?" said Daddy, as he walked over to the truck.

Mr. Perkins came out of the stable. He helped the driver lower the back of the truck. It made a little hill for the pony to walk down.

Peter and Jane came running from the Perkins

house. "Where did you get the pony?" they cried. "Is it your pony?"

Teddy was jumping up and down, singing, "We've got a pony! We've got a pony!"

"Why, Daddy!" cried Babs. "He looks just like Shorty in the circus."

"He *is* Shorty," said Daddy.

"Is it really Shorty?" asked Teddy.

"Yes," replied Daddy, stroking the pony's nose. "The circus shut down and I heard that the ponies were for sale. So I went right over and bought Shorty."

"Oh, Shorty!" cried Teddy as he threw his arms around the little pony's neck.

"Can we ride him now?" asked Babs.

"No," replied Daddy. "Shorty needs a nice rest after his trip in the truck. When his saddle comes, you can ride him."

The truck drove off and Mr. Perkins led Shorty over to a big field beside the Perkins house. He let down the bars in the fence and put Shorty in the field. Then he took off his bridle. Shorty lay right down in the tall grass and rolled on his back, kicking his legs in the air, just like a big dog.

When Shorty's saddle arrived, Mr. Perkins taught the children to ride. Soon Teddy rode so well that he was able to stay on Shorty's back when he jumped over a low hurdle.

Shorty loved the children as much as the children loved Shorty. Sometimes when they were playing on the lawn, Shorty would jump right over the fence and come trotting over to the children. The children would say, "Shake hands, Shorty," and Shorty would hold up his right hoof.

One day when Mother and Babs went into town for the mail, they saw a big poster tacked up outside of the post office. There was a picture of a horse on the poster.

"Look, Mother," said Babs, "look at the horse. What does the sign say?"

"It says there is going to be a Horse Show at the Pickwick Farms," replied Mother.

"What is a Horse Show?" asked Babs.

"It is a place where everyone takes their horses. They ride around and jump and the best horse receives a prize. The first prize is a blue ribbon."

"Are there ponies in the Horse Show?" asked Babs.

"Sometimes," answered Mother.

"Can we take Shorty?" Babs asked. "Shorty would win a blue ribbon."

"You will have to ask Daddy," said Mother.

When Babs reached home, she told Teddy what Mother had told her about the Horse Show.

"Oh, I hope Daddy will let us take Shorty," said Teddy.

The children could hardly wait until Daddy came home. As soon as they heard the car in the driveway, they ran out. "Daddy, Daddy!" they shouted. "Can we take Shorty to the Horse Show, so that he can win a blue ribbon?"

"If you can get Mr. Perkins to go with you, you may," replied Daddy.

The children were off like a shot to look for Mr. Perkins. They found him over by the apple orchard looking at the new litter of pigs.

"Mr. Perkins, Mr. Perkins!" they cried. "Will you go to the Horse Show with us, so Shorty can win a blue ribbon?"

"Sure, sure!" said Mr. Perkins. "Run along, before you frighten the pigs."

The children looked forward to the Horse Show. At last the day arrived. It had been decided that Teddy would ride Shorty at the show because he was the best rider. Daddy bought him a beautiful brown riding habit.

"How will we get Shorty over to the Horse Show?" asked Teddy.

"He will have to go in the station wagon," said Mother.

Getting Shorty into the station wagon was easier said than done. First they coaxed him.

Then they pulled him. Then they pushed him, but Shorty would not put one foot into the station wagon. At last Mr. Perkins got a pan of oats and placed it on the floor of the wagon. Now Shorty loved to eat and when he saw the pan of oats on the floor of the wagon, he walked right in. Then Mr. Perkins made his reins fast to the front seat. Teddy and Babs climbed in beside Mr. Perkins and Joe, the stable boy, stood in the back of the wagon with Shorty.

When they reached the Horse Show, they took Shorty out of the wagon and Teddy mounted him. Mr. Perkins led him over to a place that was fenced off just for ponies. Teddy sat up very straight in his little saddle and looked around him. Not very far away there were some wooden hurdles. Ladies and gentlemen, on horseback, were jumping over the hurdles. Every time a horse jumped over a hurdle, all the people who were watching clapped. Suddenly Shorty jumped over the fence and galloped toward the hurdles. Mr. Perkins ran after him. "Hold tight, Teddy!" he shouted. "Don't be afraid, Teddy!"

Shorty went right for the hurdles. His feet rose from the ground. Over the hurdle he went! Then over another and another and another.

Teddy stuck to his mount. As he took each
hurdle, the people clapped. When he finished
the crowd roared and a band began to play.
Shorty pricked up his ears. He heard the music
and started to dance just as he had danced in
the circus. How the people clapped! When the
music stopped, Shorty made a low bow and
trotted over to Mr. Perkins. Shorty looked so
proud of himself. He shook his head as if to say,
"See what I did. I'm a circus pony."

Everyone came up to shake hands with Teddy
and to tell him what a good rider he was. Then
a man came over and pinned a blue ribbon on

the side of Shorty's head. To Teddy he handed a big silver cup.

When he reached home, Teddy ran into the living room to Mother. "Look, look, Mother!" he cried. "I got a silver cup and Shorty won the blue ribbon."

"How wonderful!" said Mother, as she took the silver cup. "Did Shorty behave nicely?"

"Oh, Mother!" said Teddy. "You should have seen him!"

7

Pincushions and Pigs

It all happened on Mary the cook's birthday. In the morning Babs drove into town with Mr. Perkins to buy Mary a present. At first Babs thought she would buy Mary a new dress with red flowers on it. Then she thought perhaps a wristwatch would be better. It wouldn't wear out as soon as a dress. She had all of thirteen cents to spend so she wanted the present to be very nice.

When Mr. Perkins heard about the thirteen cents, he drove Babs right to the Five and Ten Cent Store. They wandered all around the store. There weren't any dresses or wristwatches, but there were many other things. Babs almost bought Mary a string of pearl beads. Then she thought that a bracelet would be nicer or a sparkling pin or a shiny picture frame, but when at last she came upon a counter where there was a beautiful blue satin pincushion with red roses painted on it, Babs knew that she had found Mary's birthday present. The pincushion was ten cents. Babs handed ten pennies to the girl behind the counter and watched her tie up the package.

"Now I can buy Mary something else with the three pennies," said Babs, tucking her package under her arm.

"My," said Mr. Perkins, "it's a good thing we brought the station wagon to carry all these things home."

"I'll get her three sticks of peppermint candy," said Babs.

After she bought the candy, Mr. Perkins put

her in the wagon. "You wait there," said he, "until I get the mail from the post office."

When he returned, he was carrying a large round box. "Here is a package," he said, "addressed to Miss Sarah Elizabeth Robinson. Know anybody by that name?"

Babs thought for a moment. "Why, that's me!" she cried. "That's my name! Sarah Elizabeth Robinson!"

"Oh," said Mr. Perkins, "so 'tis! Well, someone must be sending you a present."

"Oh, Mr. Perkins," cried Babs, "what do you suppose it is?"

"Don't know," said Mr. Perkins, "but it certainly looks very special."

"Let's go home right away," said Babs, "and get Mother to open it."

All the way home Babs talked of what might be in the package. When she reached the house, she rushed to Mother. "Mother," she cried, "there's a big box with my name on it. It was at the post office. Don't open it until I come back. I have to give Mary her birthday present."

Babs ran off to the kitchen. Mary was beating eggs for a cake.

"Mary," Babs called, "I've brought you a birthday present. It's a pincushion," she said, handing the package to Mary, "and some peppermint sticks."

"Now isn't that loving and kind of you to get me a birthday present!" said Mary.

Mary began to untie the package. "It's blue, Mary," said Babs, "and it has red roses painted on it."

"Well," said Mary, as she looked at her present, "it's the most beautiful pincushion I've ever seen."

Babs' face was beaming. "I have a present, too; Mother is going to open it now," she said, as she skipped out of the kitchen.

Mother cut the string on the package and removed some heavy cardboard. There was a beautiful round box. It was pink with white stripes all over it. Babs lifted the lid. It seemed to be filled with white tissue paper. She parted the sheets of paper and there, nestled inside, was a little white hat. Very carefully, she lifted it out of the box. "Oh-h-h-h!" sighed Babs. She thought she had never seen anything so beautiful as this lovely white hat. It was snowy white

and shaped like a tam-o'-shanter. Tacked to one side were some little stiff white feathers. They stuck right up straight.

"Oh, Mother," said Babs, "isn't it a pretty hat!"

"It is a beautiful hat, dear," said Mother, "and it was sweet of Grandmother Robinson to send it to you."

"Yes," said Babs, as Mother put it on her head.

Babs looked so pretty in her new white hat that she stood in front of the mirror a long time.

"You must take very good care of that lovely hat," said Mother. "You mustn't wear it around the farm."

"May I wear it on Saturday afternoons when I go to town with Daddy?" asked Babs.

"Yes, and on Sundays," replied Mother.

Mother stowed the new hat away on the shelf in Babs's closet.

In the afternoon Mother went into town. Teddy and the twins were taking turns riding Shorty. Babs couldn't stop thinking about her new hat. She longed to try it on again. At last she ran up to her room and opened the closet door. There was the pink-and-white hat box. As Babs looked up at the box, it seemed to fairly twinkle. She pulled a chair over to the closet. Climbing up, she lifted the box down. She raised the lid and peeped inside. Then she lifted the hat out and tried it on again. "It would be nice," she thought, "to take a walk in my new hat. I wouldn't go far and I would be very careful."

She went down the stairs and out of the side door. Then she trotted through the flower garden to the apple orchard. There was a stone wall that separated the flower garden from the apple orchard. Babs leaned over the stone wall. Just then she remembered that there were some new little pigs down beyond the apple orchard. She

guessed that she would go see how the pigs were coming along.

Very carefully she climbed over the stone wall and walked through the orchard. Babs forgot all about Mr. Perkins' warning that you must always be careful not to frighten little pigs. She leaned over to look at the pigs. "Hello, little pigs!" she shouted.

The pigs were so startled that they jumped. Then they set up such a squealing that Babs turned and ran. All of the pigs began running after her. Big pigs, little pigs, and middle-size

pigs, all ran pell-mell after Babs. They chased
her right through the orchard. Babs ran toward
the stone wall. If only she could get over the
wall! It looked higher than it had ever looked before. It looked so high that Babs felt that she
could never climb over it. But the pigs were after
her! Whatever could she do! She ran toward an
apple tree. Its branches were low. She had often
climbed the apple tree, so, quick as a flash, up
into the apple tree went Babs. She was out of
breath but she was safe. The pigs couldn't get her
now. She leaned over and looked down at them.

They were still squealing. All of a sudden, Babs's hat fell to the ground. No sooner had it landed than the pigs pounced upon it. The ground was damp and the pigs were muddy. Babs opened her mouth and screamed. In a moment her beautiful white hat was covered with mud. The pigs were trampling it into the ground. Babs screamed and screamed and screamed.

Mr. Perkins, who was tying up the beans, heard her. Mrs. Perkins, who was making pies, heard her. Teddy and the twins, who were in the pasture, heard her. The stable boy and all of the farmhands heard her, and Mary, who was peeling apples, heard Babs screaming. They all ran to the apple orchard.

Mr. Perkins and Mary reached the apple tree first. Babs was still screaming. "My hat, my hat, my hat," she cried.

Mary picked up the hat and Mr. Perkins lifted Babs out of the tree. He carried her, crying, back to the house. Teddy and the twins trotted along behind him. Mary carried the sorry-looking sight that was once Babs's beautiful white hat.

When they reached the house, Mother had

just returned. The children told her what had happened down in the apple orchard.

Mother took Babs upstairs. She washed her red swollen eyes. "You see, Babs," she said, "this is what happens when little girls are disobedient. Your pretty white hat is ruined."

Babs couldn't stop crying. She lay down on her bed and sobbed. After a while, Mary came

in to see her. "Now come," said Mary, "dry your tears, for you're spoiling Mary's birthday. That beautiful blue pincushion you gave me this morning, why, I can't enjoy it with my little Babs crying like this. You don't want to spoil Mary's birthday, do you?"

Babs gulped. "No," she said, "but I spoiled my hat."

"Well, now!" said Mary. "I'll see what I can do with it. Perhaps I can clean it up."

"But the little feathers," said Babs. "I saw the pigs tear the little feathers all to pieces."

"Just go to sleep," said Mary, "and leave it all to Mary."

The next morning when Babs woke up, Mary was standing in the doorway. She was holding the white hat. It looked fresh and clean again and there were the stiff little white feathers sticking up on one side.

"Oh, Mary," cried Babs, "where did you get the feathers?"

"Well," said Mary, "I went down to the barnyard and I said to the big white rooster, 'Come along here, and give us a couple of white feathers for Babs's hat.' And he walked right over and dropped two feathers at my feet. And here's your little hat, almost as good as new."

"Oh, Mary!" cried Babs. "You're wonderful! Do you still like your pincushion?"

"My pincushion!" said Mary. "It's the most beautiful pincushion in all the world!"

8

What the Explorers Brought Home

Teddy and Babs and the twins lay in the tall grass in the meadow. It was a warm, sunny afternoon. Jane was watching the white, fleecy clouds chase each other across the blue sky. Teddy was looking at an ant that was climbing up a blade of grass. Floppy and Whiskers lay curled up in balls. They were enjoying an afternoon nap.

"Let's do something," said Peter.

"What shall we do?" asked Jane.

"We could pick blueberries," said Babs.

"Aw, I'm tired of picking blueberries," said Teddy. "Every time we go out, you want to pick blueberries."

"Let's play we're explorers," said Peter.

"What's 'splorers'?" asked Babs.

"Explorers are people who go out and find things," said Peter, "like Christopher Columbus. He went out in a big ship and found America."

"Well, what will we find?" said Teddy.

"Oh, you don't know what you're going to find," said Peter. "It's always a surprise."

"Like Christopher Columbus?" asked Babs.

"Sure," said Peter, "like Christopher Columbus. He was awful surprised when he found America."

"Where shall we go to explore?" asked Jane.

"Let's go up the hill to the woods," said Peter. "We can make-believe it's a new country and that we have never been there before."

"I thought we were going in a boat," said Babs, "like Christopher Columbus."

"Oh, you don't have to go in a boat," said Peter. "You can explore on the land. You just walk until you discover something you never saw before."

"All right," said Teddy, "let's be explorers."

The children started up the hill. They walked one behind the other. Floppy and Whiskers ran ahead, sniffing here and there.

When the children reached the woods, Teddy said, "You know, we should have guns. Explorers always have guns."

"Why?" said Babs.

"Because they might meet wild animals," replied Peter. "Explorers always bring home bears and things."

Teddy picked up a long stick. "This is my gun," he said. "I'll shoot any old bear that comes along."

After a while Jane found a long stick. "I have a gun, too," she said, putting it over her shoulder.

"You wouldn't shoot a baby bear, would you?" asked Babs.

"No, just big grizzlies," replied Teddy.

"We could take it home and use the skin for a rug," said Jane.

Soon Peter and Babs found sticks that they could use for guns. The four children tramped on through the woods.

"Do you think we will find anything?" asked Babs.

"Course we'll find something," said Peter. "Explorers always find something."

Just then Floppy and Whiskers stopped still. They lifted their heads and sniffed. Their noses twitched. *Sniff! Sniff! Sniff!* Then their noses went down to the ground. *Sniff! Sniff! Sniff!* Like a flash they were off. The children left the path to follow the dogs. In a few moments the dogs began to bark. Peter ran ahead. When he reached the dogs, he found them standing over a little animal. The animal lay beside an old tree stump.

"Oh, look!" cried Peter, as the other children appeared. "Look at the little animal. Somebody must have shot it with a real gun."

Floppy began to shake the animal.

"Drop it, Floppy!" cried Peter. "Leave it alone."

Floppy dropped it. The children stooped down to examine the animal.

"What do you suppose it is?" asked Jane.

"Maybe it's a baby bear," said Babs.

"No," replied Peter, "it isn't a baby bear. Bears don't have white stripes on their backs."

"It has a pretty skin," said Teddy, stroking the fur.

"It smells funny," said Jane.

"I don't smell anything," said Peter.

"Let's take it home," said Teddy.

"Yes," said Peter, "maybe Grandaddy could skin it for us."

"It would make my doll a fur coat," said Jane.

"Do you think I could have the tail for my bicycle?" asked Teddy.

"I guess so," said Peter. "It was your dog that found it."

"Well, let's take it home, anyway," said Jane. "We're explorers and we can make-believe we're bringing home a bear."

"Can I carry it?" said Babs. "I would like to carry it."

Peter picked up the animal and placed it in Babs's arms.

"I think it's terrible to shoot little animals," said Babs, almost in tears.

The children started for home. They had gone far into the woods so that it was a long way back. Soon Babs grew tired of carrying the little animal. "Here, Jane," she said, "you carry it a while."

Jane took the animal. "I think it smells sort of funny," said Jane.

"Aw, girls are fussy," said Peter, "always thinking about how things smell."

"Well, then, you carry it," said Jane, handing it to Peter.

Peter carried the animal a long way. Finally Teddy said, "I would like to carry it a little while, Peter."

"All right," said Peter.

When the little party reached home, Teddy was carrying the animal close against his chest. As they neared the house they could see Mr. Perkins mowing the grass by the driveway.

"Oh, Grandaddy," cried Peter, "look what we found in the woods!"

"We've been sploring!" shouted Babs.

"We've brought home a bear," cried Teddy.

Mr. Perkins left his lawn mower and came toward the children.

"Gracious! Goodness!" he cried. "What have you brought home!"

Teddy held up the animal.

"Oh, my stars and buttons!" shouted Mr. Perkins. "It's a skunk! Can't you smell it? Oh, my goodness! Whatever made you bring home a skunk!"

"It's pretty, Grandaddy," said Peter. "We thought that you could skin it for us."

"Jumping junipers!" cried Mr. Perkins. "Put it in this basket and don't go in the house. You could smell the four of you in seven states. Sit right down on this bench until I come back."

Teddy dropped the skunk into an old basket. Then the children sat down in a row on the

bench. They were so surprised they couldn't think of anything to say, so they just sat still, swinging their legs.

Mr. Perkins went into the house. When he returned, Mrs. Perkins was with him. "Land sakes!" cried Mrs. Perkins. "I never smelled anything so awful. We'll have to burn their clothes and give them baths before they can go into the house."

Mr. Perkins brought out an old wooden washtub and placed it under the outdoor faucet at the back of the house. When the tub was full of water, Mrs. Perkins said, "Come now, you two boys, take off your clothes and get into this tub."

"You mean we have to take off our clothes out here?" said Peter.

"Yes, every stitch," said Mrs. Perkins.

Teddy and Peter took their clothes off and Mr. Perkins picked them up with the end of a pole and dropped them in a wire can.

"Now, get in the tub," said Mrs. Perkins.

Peter and Teddy stepped into the tub and Mrs. Perkins began scrubbing them with a brush and some soap. She scrubbed them all over. Then she washed their hair.

Jane and Babs sat on the bench waiting for their turn.

When Mrs. Perkins was through with the boys, she gave them each a towel. Peter ran indoors and Teddy ran across the road to his house.

"Come along now," Mrs. Perkins called to the two little girls.

The little girls took off their clothes while Mrs. Perkins filled the tub a second time. Again, Mr. Perkins picked up the little pile of clothes with the end of the pole. When he had dropped them into the can, he put a match to the clothes. In a few minutes there were just a few ashes.

Jane and Babs stepped into the tub and Mrs. Perkins set to work again with her brush and soap. She washed their hair and rinsed it under the faucet. Then she gave them each a towel and sent them scampering.

When Babs ran through the kitchen door, Mary threw up her hands. "Goodness!" she cried, "First, one of you comes running in without a stitch on and now here comes another. What did you do with your clothes?"

"Mr. Perkins burned them," said Babs, as she tramped up the back stairs.

Outside, Mrs. Perkins emptied the tub. "Well, that's over," she said.

Just then, Floppy and Whiskers appeared. They ran to Mrs. Perkins.

"Phew!" said Mrs. Perkins, "I declare you smell worse than the children."

Once more she filled the tub. Then she picked up Floppy and Whiskers and put them in the water. She scrubbed the little dogs, just as she had scrubbed the children. At last she lifted them out of the water. The dogs shook themselves very hard. Then they ran up and down the lawn and rolled on the newly cut grass.

Meanwhile, Mr. Perkins dug a deep hole and buried the skunk.

After dinner, the four children were sitting on the porch step. They looked like shiny new pennies in their clean clothes. Jane's hair was still damp.

"What did your grandaddy say that little animal was?" asked Babs.

"It was a skunk," said Peter.

"I told you it smelled funny," said Jane.

"I guess it did," said Peter.

"Well, we went exploring," said Teddy, "and we brought something home with us."

9

What Happened
to the Only Pear

Close to the side porch of the Robinsons' house there grew a pear tree. It was a very special kind of pear tree and Mr. Robinson was very proud of it. He would always say to visitors, "This is a very fine pear tree. There isn't another like it for miles around. I am looking forward to having some good pears."

The visitors would always nod their heads

and look very wise as though they knew all about pear trees.

In the spring the pear tree was covered with lovely white blossoms, but a late frost nipped them. Mr. Perkins said it was too bad, because it meant that the tree would not bear much fruit.

For a long time, it looked as though there were not going to be any pears, but one day Babs saw a tiny green pear hanging from one of the branches. She called Teddy to look at it.

"Sure 'nuff," said Teddy. "That's a pear, all right."

Off they ran to spread the news. Everyone was excited about the one pear.

Week after week, the children watched the pear grow. Teddy called it "Daddy's pear," because Daddy said that he didn't want anything to happen to it.

The pear grew larger and larger. By September it was so big and heavy that it almost touched the porch roof. The pear was no longer green but a pale yellow. It showed very plainly against the green leaves. Babs could see it from her bedroom window. *If my arm was as long as a giraffe's neck, I could reach right out the*

window and pick the pear, thought Babs. But Babs knew that Daddy had said that no one should pick the pear.

Every time the children walked under the pear tree, they would look up at the pear. Sometimes they would jump and make-believe to pick it. Now that it was almost ripe, it didn't look as far away as it had when it was green.

One day the children were lying on the grass under the tree.

"You know what!" said Peter. "I'll bet if I stood on a ladder, I could reach that pear."

"Well, you better not," said Teddy. "Daddy

says that no one is to pick that pear. It's Daddy's pear."

"Do you suppose it's soft yet?" said Jane.

"It looks soft," said Babs.

A few days later Teddy and Babs and Peter came round the corner of the house. "Jane! Oh, Jane!" they called.

There was no answer.

"Where do you s'pose she is?" said Peter.

"Jane! Oh, Jane!" they cried. There was still no answer.

The children sat down under the pear tree. "That's funny," said Teddy. "Where do you suppose Jane went?"

"Maybe she went to the post office with your grandaddy," said Babs.

Teddy lay down on his back. "Why, there she is," he cried, "up in the pear tree!"

"Say, what are you doing up in the pear tree?" Peter called.

"I was just hiding, that was all," said Jane.

"I'll bet you were feeling that pear," said Babs.

"Well, it isn't soft yet," said Jane.

"You better leave Daddy's pear alone," said Teddy.

"I didn't hurt it," said Jane, as she climbed down.

"Did you smell it?" asked Babs.

"No, but I'll bet in another week it will be ripe," replied Jane.

"What do you suppose your daddy is going to do with it?" said Peter.

"I don't know," said Teddy. "I guess he's going to eat it."

The pear grew lovelier every day. One side turned a beautiful pink. Daddy warned the children again that they were not to pick the pear.

One day Mother went to the city. Teddy and Babs spent the morning playing trains on the stairs. Teddy's Uncle Bill had sent him a brand-new ticket puncher. Teddy went up and down the stairs punching the tickets of all the dolls and stuffed animals who were riding on the train. Sometimes he would let Babs be the conductor and she would punch the tickets. After a while Babs called out, "There goes Peter! I wonder where he is going with that little ladder?"

Teddy rushed to the door. "Peter," he called, "do you want to come and play?"

Peter didn't answer. Teddy ran after him. "Peter!" he cried. "Wait for me."

Peter turned round and waited for Teddy. "What were you doing with the ladder?" asked Teddy.

"Oh, I just needed it to get my ball," replied Peter.

"I've got a new ticket puncher," said Teddy.

"Can I punch with it?" asked Peter, as he stood the ladder in the toolshed.

The two little boys sat down behind the toolshed to look at the ticket puncher.

Babs went upstairs to her room. She decided to change her best doll's dress. It was really very dirty. Babs took off all of her doll's clothes. Then she gave her a bath and dried her with a towel. After she was dressed in fresh, clean clothes, she looked very beautiful. Babs set her on the windowsill. Then she looked out of the window. The sun was shining on the sloping roof of the porch. It was a lovely warm September sun. Not hot like the summer sun. Babs suddenly thought it would be lovely to be on the porch roof. She had never thought of doing this before, but now she opened the screen and stepped out of the window. She lay down. It was nice to feel the warm sunshine on her arms and legs. She stayed quite a long time.

After a while Babs heard Jane calling her. Jane had spied her on the roof. "What are you doing up on the roof?" said Jane.

"Oh, nothing!" replied Babs. "I'm coming down now."

Babs climbed in the window and ran downstairs to Jane.

After lunch, Babs drove into town with Mr. Perkins. Teddy and Peter went off to the brook to run Peter's toy motorboat.

Jane didn't want to get her new blue-and-white striped dress dirty, so she decided to color pictures. She lay down under the pear tree and set to work.

Sometime later, Teddy came back from the brook alone. He had come back to get his little toy canoe. Jane was gone. There was no one around. As he went into the house, he could hear a fly buzzing on the screen door. The house seemed very quiet.

Teddy went upstairs to his room. He found the little canoe on his mantelshelf. Then he wandered over to Babs's room. There didn't seem to be a soul in the house. The screen was still open at the window. Teddy walked over to the window and looked out.

Meanwhile, Peter sat beside the brook. He wondered what Teddy could be doing. He had been gone such a long time. Peter threw stones into the brook. Then he watched a frog catching flies. Finally, he decided to go home. When he reached the house, Jane was in the kitchen helping her grandmother to cut cookies. "Did you see Teddy?" asked Peter.

"No," replied Jane. "I haven't seen him all afternoon."

About five o'clock, Mother came back from the city. The children were nowhere in sight. She walked out on the porch. "I wonder where they are," she thought.

Just then she looked up into the pear tree. She looked for the pear. The beautiful pear was gone. There, hanging from the branch over the roof of the porch, was the core of the pear. The rest of it had been eaten away. She could still see the marks of little teeth. Just as she was turning away from the tree, she saw a piece of blue-and-white striped material hanging from a limb. "Oh!" said Mother. "I see! The one who ate the pear was wearing blue and white stripes." She took the little rag off the tree.

"Teddy!" she called. "Babs! Where are you?"
All was quiet.

At last, Teddy came up from the pasture and Babs came back from town.

Mother sent Teddy for Peter and Jane. When the four children had gathered around Mrs. Robinson, she said, "Children, something terrible has happened."

She pointed up into the tree. The children looked up at the core of the pear. "Oh!" they gasped, and their faces were very grave.

"Jane," said Mrs. Robinson, "is this a piece of your dress?"

"Yes, Mrs. Robinson," said Jane.

"Did you climb up into the pear tree today?" Mrs. Robinson asked.

"Yes, I did," replied Jane, "but I didn't eat the pear."

Jane looked at Babs. "Babs, you were up on the roof this morning; I'll bet you ate it."

"Did you eat it, Babs?" asked Mother.

"No, Mother," said Babs, "but I saw Peter with a little ladder this morning."

"Peter," said Mrs. Robinson, "did you do it?"

"No, Mrs. Robinson," answered Peter. "I just

had the ladder to get my ball. It went up on the windowsill."

Mrs. Robinson turned to Teddy. "Teddy," she said, "did you pick the pear?"

Teddy hung his head.

"Teddy," said Mother, "didn't Daddy tell you that you were not to pick that pear?"

"But, Mother," said Teddy, "I didn't pick it, I only ate it."

Mother marched Teddy upstairs. She put him right to bed. When dinnertime came, she brought him a bowl of cereal. "Can't I have any dessert?" asked Teddy.

"No," replied Mother, "you had your dessert when you ate Daddy's pear."

"Is Daddy very angry with me?" asked Teddy.

"Very," said Mother.

"What do you think he will do to me?" Teddy asked.

"I don't know," answered Mother.

Teddy lay alone in the dark. He could hear Mother and Daddy talking downstairs. Sometimes he could hear Babs. He felt very lonely. Pretty soon, he heard Babs go to bed.

A long time afterwards he heard Mother and

Daddy come upstairs. He wondered whether Daddy would come in and sit on his bed. He always did. Teddy waited and waited. All the lights were out now. The house was so quiet Teddy could hear the clock tick. "Daddy isn't coming," thought Teddy. "He isn't coming. Daddy is going to stay cross with me all night." Teddy began to cry. He wished, oh, how he wished, he had not eaten the pear!

After a while, Teddy got up and tiptoed to the door of Daddy's room. He opened the door. "Daddy!" he called, very softly. "Daddy!"

"Yes, Teddy," replied Daddy.

"I can't go to sleep, Daddy," said Teddy. "Can I come in your bed?"

"Come on," said Daddy.

Teddy climbed into bed with Daddy. He snuggled up close beside him. "Daddy," he said, "I'll give you my new ticket puncher."

"Thanks, Teddy," replied Daddy.

"It's a very nice ticket puncher," said Teddy. "It punches little holes shaped like stars. I'll give you anything of mine you want, Daddy."

Daddy put his arm around his little boy.

"Daddy," said Teddy, "I didn't know that I was going to eat it. The window was open and I

just thought that I would like to smell it. So I climbed out and it smelled so good, I thought I would take just a little tiny bite, where it wouldn't show. And then I took another bite and pretty soon it was all gone."

"Yes," said Daddy, "that is the way naughty things happen."

"Will you forgive me this time, Daddy?"

"Yes," said Daddy, "I'll forgive you. Now go to sleep."

"Daddy," said Teddy, "it was an awful good pear."

10

End of Summer

The days were growing shorter, and the leaves on the trees were beginning to turn red and yellow. Teddy and Babs and the twins no longer played out-of-doors after dinner. They gathered in front of the open fire and popped corn and toasted marshmallows. Every-day they could see great flocks of birds flying toward the south.

One day Peter said, "Pretty soon Jane and I will be flying south. We have to go back to school soon. Wouldn't it be fun if we could just ride on one of those birds instead of going in the train? I'll bet they fly right over our house."

"I think it's fun to go on the train," said Jane. "I like to listen to the engine. It always says, *Got chur trunk! Got chur trunk! Got chur trunk!*"

"Is it very far to where you live?" asked Teddy.

"It's pretty far," said Peter.

"We have to take our lunch with us," said Jane. "Grandmother always gives us a good lunch to eat on the train."

"Do you go all by yourselves?" asked Babs.

"Yes," replied Jane, "all by ourselves."

"Oh, Grandaddy puts us on the train and he tells the conductor to take care of us. Then the conductor puts us off at Washington and our daddy is always there to meet us."

"That must be fun," said Teddy. "I would like that."

"Well, it won't be long now before we'll go," said Jane.

When the day arrived for the twins to leave,

there was a great deal of excitement. Grandmother had packed their trunk the day before and Grandaddy had taken it to the station in the station wagon. Now Peter and Jane kept finding things that they wanted to take home with them.

"Oh, Grandmother!" cried Jane. "Here's my doll, Hannah, and all of her clothes. What shall I do with her?"

"Dear, dear!" said Grandmother. "Hannah and her clothes should have gone in the trunk. Now you will have to carry her."

"Grandmother!" Peter called. "I have to take my gun and my new fishing rod. Daddy might take me fishing someday."

"Well, Grandaddy will have to wrap them up for you," said Grandmother.

Just then Jane came running into the kitchen. "Grandmother! Grandmother!" she panted. "What do you think Mary gave me for a going-away present?"

"I can't imagine," said Grandmother.

"She gave me her canary bird. The cage and everything."

"Well, I don't see how you'll be able to go on the train with a birdcage," said Grandmother.

"Oh, I can carry it," said Jane.

Grandmother was busy making sandwiches. She packed the twins' lunch in a big square box. There were three kinds of sandwiches and cookies and hard-boiled eggs. There were plums and two big round peppermint patties. There was a big banana for each of them and some peanut-butter crackers.

"Now, do be careful, when you eat your lunch, not to drop papers on the floor. Let the people on the train see that you know how to mind your manners," said Grandmother.

The children promised to be very careful.

After a while, Peter burst into the kitchen. "Look, Grandmother!" he cried. "Teddy says I can take Barney home with me. He says he's mine to keep." Peter was carrying a great big turtle.

"Now, you can't take a turtle on the train with you," said Grandmother.

"Why not, Grandmother? He wouldn't be any trouble," said Peter. "I can get Grandaddy to put him in a box with holes punched in the lid."

"Well, go talk to your grandaddy about it," said Grandmother.

Peter rushed out, carrying his turtle.

When it was time to leave for the train, Mr. Perkins drove the station wagon up to the front door. Teddy and Babs were on the front seat. They were going to the station to see the twins off. Mrs. Robinson and Mary, the cook, and Joe, the stable boy, were gathered round the wagon to say good-bye to the twins. Grandaddy put their traveling bag in the wagon. He put the birdcage in and the gun and the fishing rod.

Grandmother came rushing out of the door. "Here," she said, "don't forget this chocolate cake I baked for your mother. Jane, be sure to carry it very carefully."

"Teddy, you're going without your coat," called Grandaddy.

At last they were ready. They kissed everyone good-bye. The wagon started. "Good-bye! Good-bye!" they called.

Everyone waved. "Good-bye, Jane!" they called. "Good-bye, Peter!"

They hadn't gone very far when Peter cried, "Grandaddy! I forgot my turtle. We'll have to go back for Barney."

Grandaddy turned the car around and drove

back to the house. Peter jumped out. He ran into the kitchen. "I forgot my turtle," he shouted.

He picked up the box and in a moment he was back in the wagon.

Off they started again. They had to go all the way into town to the station because the through train didn't stop at the little station nearby. Only the milk train stopped there early in the morning.

They drove along the dirt road in a cloud of dust until they turned onto the main highway. Jake's gasoline station was on the corner. Jake ran out when he saw the station wagon. He waved wildly. The children waved too. "Goodbye," they called, "good-bye."

Jake ran after them, waving. The children waved until they could see him no longer.

The wagon flew over the smooth road. In a few moments a policeman on a motorcycle drove up beside the wagon. The policeman motioned for Mr. Perkins to drive over to the side of the road. Mr. Perkins drew up and stopped the wagon.

"Is your name Perkins?" asked the officer.

"Yes," said Mr. Perkins.

"Well, you forgot your lunch," said the officer.

Mr. Perkins's mouth dropped open; he was so surprised. "How do you know?" he asked.

"Your wife telephoned to Jake at the gas station. She told him to stop you, but you didn't pay any attention to him. Just then, I came along, so he sent me after you."

"Thank you very much," said Mr. Perkins.

Once more he turned the wagon around and started back to the farm.

"He was a nice policeman, wasn't he?" said Jane. "It would be terrible to go without our lunch."

"It will be terrible if you miss your train," said Grandaddy.

He drove as fast as he could over the dirt road. As they swung into the drive, Grandmother came running to meet them. She handed the lunch box to Teddy and Grandaddy turned the wagon around. Back they went to the highway. Grandaddy looked at his watch. "We'll never make that train," he said. "You'll miss it sure as my name is Perkins."

"Oh, Grandaddy!" cried Jane. "What shall we do!"

"There's nothing to do but go to the little station where they load the milk and see if we can flag the train."

"Do you think they will stop?" asked Teddy.

"I don't know for sure, but we can try it," said Grandaddy.

Mr. Perkins turned onto the road that led to the little station. "She's due to pass there in fifteen minutes," he said.

"What shall we use to flag the train, Grandaddy?" asked Jane.

"I don't know," said Grandaddy. "We ought to have something red."

"I've got on red socks," said Jane. "I'll take one off." Jane slipped off her shoe and took off her sock.

When they reached the station, they still had five minutes before the train was due.

"Now, I'll do the waving," said Grandaddy. "You children stand back in the shed where it is safe. After all, the train may go by."

All of a sudden, there was a sharp whistle. "Here she comes!" shouted Grandaddy. Peter could feel himself tingling with excitement. Jane's knees felt wobbly.

The children ran back in the shed and

Grandaddy ran along beside the track toward the train. He was waving Jane's sock.

The children could hear the train now, rushing toward them. Then they heard the screech of the brakes and the train slowed up and stopped at the station.

The children rushed forward. A conductor jumped down. Mr. Perkins pushed the children up the steps. Jane clutched her doll under one arm and held the chocolate cake in the other.

"Mr. Perkins will meet these children at Washington," said Grandaddy, as he handed up all the boxes and bags and packages.

"All right, sir," said the conductor. "Don't worry about them. I'll deliver them to their father. I know these children; I brought them up here in June."

Peter and Jane stood on the platform with the conductor. The train began to pull away from the station. "Good-bye!" they called. "Good-bye, Grandaddy! Good-bye, Teddy and Babs!"

"Good-bye," shouted Teddy and Babs.

"Good-bye!" called Grandaddy.

In a moment the train was out of sight.

"Oh, Mr. Perkins!" cried Babs, "you forgot to give Jane her sock."

Turn the page for a peek at another
Carolyn Haywood classic

Here's a Penny

where Penny is really in luck!

1

A Brand-New Penny

They called him Penny. His name wasn't
Penn or Penrose or Penrod or anything that
would make you think of Penny. His real name
was William.

Before Penny came to live with his daddy and
mother, his daddy had said, "When we get our
little boy, let's name him William. Then we can
call him Bill."

"Not Billy?" asked Mother.

"Not Billy, nor Willy, nor anything else that ends in *ee*. Just plain Bill," said Daddy.

"Very well!" replied Mother. "Plain Bill it shall be."

But this is how he happened to be called Penny.

Long before Penny arrived, his mother and daddy decided that more than anything else in the world they wanted a little boy.

"A little red-haired boy," his mother used to say.

"With freckles on his nose," Daddy would add. And then Mother and Daddy would look at each other and laugh, just because they had said it so many times.

One day Daddy received a telegram from the head of a big hospital. It said that they had some babies that needed fathers and mothers, so Mother and Daddy got right on the train and went to see the babies.

They looked at the babies, one by one. They were all sweet and cuddly. There was one with black hair and one with hair like a fuzzy peach and there was one with no hair at all.

"Maybe it will be red when he gets it," said Daddy.

"No," replied Mother, "we have to be sure."

And then she spied Penny. He was sound asleep in his little basket. He was the color of a ripe apricot and his head was covered with red gold ringlets.

"Here he is!" whispered Mother. "Here's our little boy!"

Daddy looked at him very carefully. "Is that a freckle on his nose?" he asked.

Mother leaned over and looked at the tiny button of a nose. "I think it will be, by the time he is six," she replied.

Mother picked him up and the sunlight fell on the baby's head.

"My goodness!" said Daddy. "He looks like a brand-new copper penny."

Mother cradled the baby in her arms. He opened his eyes and stretched his mouth into a funny toothless grin. "He's just a dear, precious little penny," she said.

And so they named him William. But they called him Penny.

Now, Penny was six years old with freckles on his nose. He was in the first grade and he loved to go to school.

Patsy, the little girl next door, was in the

first grade, too. Every morning Penny would
stand on his toes and lift the brass knocker on
Patsy's front door. Then he would hear Patsy's
feet pattering, and in a moment she would
pop out of the door. Then off to school they
tramped.

One morning Penny was full of excitement.
"I'm going to get a kitten," he said, the moment
Patsy appeared.

"How do you know you are?" asked Patsy.

"My mother said I could get one," replied Penny. "He's going to be a black kitten, with a white nose and white paws."

"How do you know?" asked Patsy.

"'Cause that's the kind I want," said Penny.

"Well, you can't always get kittens just the way you want 'em," said Patsy. "You have to take 'em the way they come."

"Who said so?" asked Penny.

"My mommy said so," replied Patsy.

"Well, anyway, my kitten's going to be a black kitten, with a white nose and white paws," said Penny.

"I wish I could have a kitten," said Patsy.

"Why don't you get one?" asked Penny.

"My mommy won't let me have one," answered Patsy. "She says she doesn't like cats."

"I'll let you play with mine sometimes," said Penny.

"I want one of my own," said Patsy, kicking a pebble. "I think it's mean of you to get a kitten when I can't have one."

Patsy pouted and there were tears in her eyes. After a while she said, "Well, anyway, I'm my mommy and daddy's real little girl."

Penny didn't know what that had to do with kittens, so he didn't say anything.

Patsy stood still and looked at Penny. "I said, 'I'm my mommy and daddy's real little girl,'" she said in a very loud voice.

Penny just looked at Patsy. He didn't know what he was supposed to say, so he just said, "Uh-huh."

"But you're not your mommy and daddy's real little boy," shouted Patsy.

Penny felt his cheeks grow hot. "I am so Mother and Daddy's real little boy," he replied.

"Oh, no you're not!" cried Patsy. "You're just 'dopted."

"I know I'm 'dopted," said Penny. "My mother told me so. But I'm her real little boy."

"No, you're not," said Patsy. "You can't be. Not really truly."

Penny turned away from Patsy and ran. He wanted to get away from her as fast as he could.

"Not really truly!" cried Patsy. "Not really truly!"

Penny ran faster. Patsy was way behind him now but he could still hear her calling, "Not really truly!"

Penny's little legs flew. His cheeks were hot

and his ears were bright red. He never looked back to see where Patsy was.

When he reached the school, he went right into his classroom. He didn't even stop to say good morning to Miss Roberts, his teacher. He went right to his desk and took out his scrapbook. He made believe that he was very busy. He was really blinking his eyes to keep back the tears. He had to bite his lip to keep it from trembling.

When Patsy came in, Penny didn't look at her. He didn't look at her once all morning. Over and over in his head he could hear her calling, "Not really truly! Not really truly!"

Once Miss Roberts said, "What is the matter with Penny today? He doesn't look very shiny."

Penny didn't look up. He just hammered a nail very hard. He was building a bed for Judy, the big doll that belonged to the first grade. He could hardly wait for school to be over. He wanted to go home to Mother. He wanted her very, very badly.

At last the bell rang. Penny was the first one out of the door. He didn't wait for Patsy. He ran faster and faster and faster all the way home.

The back door was open. Penny dashed in.

Minnie, the cook, was baking cookies. "Land sakes!" she cried. "You look ready to burst."

"Where's Mother?" gasped Penny.

"Upstairs," said Minnie.

Penny stomped up the stairs. "Mother," he called. "Mother, where are you?"

Mother was sitting in the study, darning Daddy's socks. When she saw Penny's face, she dropped the sock. Penny threw himself into his mother's arms. The tears that he had kept back all morning rolled down his cheeks. His mother's arms held him tight. "There, there," she murmured. "Tell Mother what's the matter."

It was a long time before Penny could speak. He just cried and cried and the tears made his

mother's neck all wet. She held him close and said in a very soft voice, "Tell Mother, Penny. Tell Mother what it is."

At last Penny seemed to run out of tears. "Patsy says I'm not your really truly little boy," he gulped.

"Patsy is mistaken," said his mother, wiping his eyes.

"She says when you're 'dopted you can't be really truly," said Penny.

"Nonsense!" said Mother. "There is only one thing that makes a little boy 'really truly.'"

Penny sat up and looked at his mother. His blue eyes were big and round. Teardrops still hung on his eyelashes. "What does, Mother?" he said.

"Why, his mother's love for him," said Mother. "His mother's love for him makes him her really truly little boy."

"And does his daddy's love for him make him his really truly little boy?" asked Penny.

"It certainly does," replied Mother.

Then his mother told him how she and Daddy had talked about him long before he arrived. How they looked for just the little boy they wanted, with red hair and freckles on his nose.

Penny snuggled into his mother's neck. "Did you look at other little boys?" he asked.

"Indeed, yes," said Mother.

"But they didn't suit, did they?" said Penny.

"No. They were very nice," said Mother, "but we waited until we found you. And you were just what we wanted."

"That's the way I'm going to 'dopt my kitten," said Penny. "I'm going to wait until I find a black one with a white nose and white paws. And I'll love him so much that he'll be my really truly kitten."

"Of course," said Mother.

"I guess I'll go get a cookie," said Penny, as he slid off of his mother's lap.

When he reached the door he turned around. "I guess I'll take a cookie over to Patsy," he said. "And I'll tell her she's mistaken."

CAROLYN HAYWOOD (1898–1990) was born in Philadelphia and began her career as an artist. She hoped to become a children's book illustrator, but at an editor's suggestion, she began writing stories about the everyday lives of children. The first of those, *"B" Is for Betsy,* was published in 1939, and more than fifty other books followed. One of America's most popular authors for children, Ms. Haywood used many of her own childhood experiences in her novels. "I write for children," she once explained, "because I feel that they need to know what is going on in their world and they can best understand it through stories."